Usborne

Phonics Readers

Sam sheep can't sleep

Phil Roxbee Cox

Illustrated by Stephen Cartwright

Edited by Jenny Tyler

Language consultant: Marlynne Grant
BSc, CertEd, MEdPsych, PhD, AFBPs, CPsychol

There is a little yellow duck to find on every page.

First published in 2006 by Usborne Publishing Ltd., Usborne House, 83-85 Saffron Hill, London EC1N 8RT, England. www.usborne.com

Printed in China. UE. First published in America in 2006.

Sam Sheep can't sleep.

Sam Sheep gets up.

Sam Sheep wakes up Pup.

Pup barks. "It's late. It's dark."

"Go to sleep, Sam Sheep!"

"I can't sleep," says Sam Sheep.
"I need to see Fat Cat."

"Fat Cat can sleep for weeks and weeks!"

Fat Cat's on her sleeping mat in the park.
Pup barks.

"It's late. It's dark. Go to sleep!"
"Sorry," barks Pup. "Sam Sheep can't sleep."

"You need to see Ted in his red bed."

Ted is asleep in his red bed.

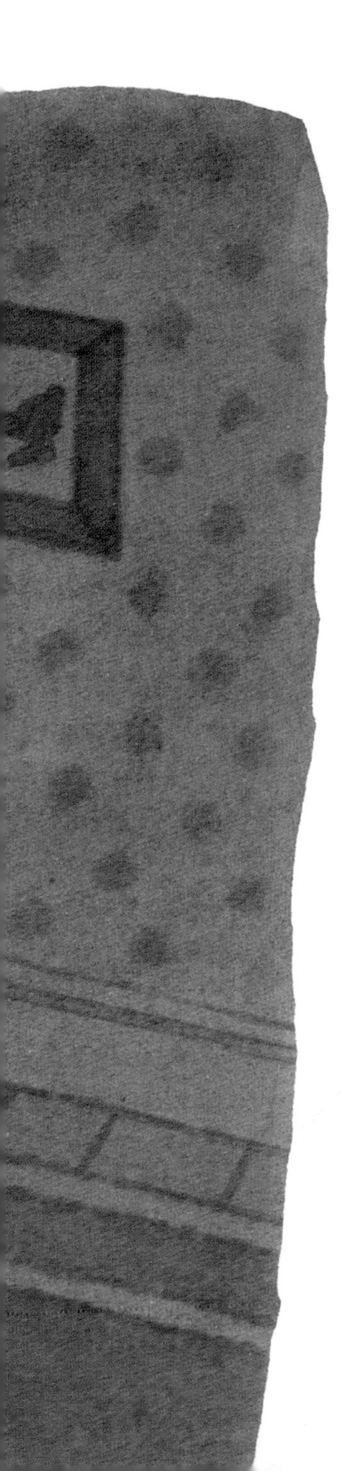

Pup barks in the
dark night ...

"You gave me a fright!"

"Sorry," barks Pup. "Sam Sheep can't sleep."

"Then let's see Big Pig, down the street."

Big Pig grunts "You woke me up!"
Fat Cat yawns. "Don't blame us."

"Sorry," barks Pup. "Sam Sheep can't sleep."

"Can't sleep?" says Big Pig. "Then do a jig."

"That will make you sleep, Sam Sheep."

So Pup starts to jiggle.

Fat Cat starts to wiggle.

Ted does a wriggle.

But what about Sam Sheep?

Sam Sheep is asleep!